Empyrean *Summer 2025*

A QUARTERLY OF ARTS AND LITERATURE
PUBLISHED INDEPENDENTLY

Editor-in-Chief

Kaylyn Dunn

Sponsored by

Kada's Bookstore

Special Additions by

Mel Einhorn

https://www.empyreanliterarymagazine.com/

To submit, go to:
www.empyreanliterarymagazine.com/generalsubmissions

Contents

Introduction

IN THE quiet moments of reflection, we often find ourselves pondering whether our lives are authored by an unseen hand or are the result of chance encounters and random events. Is there a cosmic blueprint that guides our steps or are we merely passengers on a turbulent river? These questions have fueled philosophical debates, religious doctrines, and literary masterpieces, each attempting to unravel the threads of our existence.

Throughout history, writers and thinkers have grappled with these themes—poets whispering of stars aligning, novelists charting characters caught in the web of their own fates, philosophers contemplating the balance between control and surrender. Their words remind us that the tension between fate and free will is not merely a philosophical quandary but a deeply personal experience. It influences our choices, our hopes, and our fears.

In this collection, you will find stories that delve into the intricate dance between destiny and choice, poems that meditate on the unseen forces shaping our lives, essays that challenge us to reconsider notions of control, and reflections that seek to find meaning amid uncertainty. Together, these works invite us to consider: Are we destined to follow a predetermined path, or do we forge our own way through acts of courage and conviction? Can understanding the nature of fate provide solace, or does it impose a burden of inevitability?

Thank you for joining us in this exploration. May the stories and reflections within inspire you to reflect on your own path, all of its twists, turns, and the unseen forces that shape your destiny.

Final Thoughts

1st Place Poetry Winner   Mel Einhorn

I feel a permeating sadness like the corona of a
moon,
Or a sun fading into another medium.
As grandchildren, tied to parents play
Run about and ride energetic waves, and spring
hovers,
They pass me as if I were invisible,
While I am bursting into sharing things
They may remember when I'm gone,
Unlike grandma who seems
More likely to beget a memory, not a tenuous relic.

The tides of my life are blessed.
Spared from a tortuous heritage which survivors
often choose to obscure.
Challenged by naysayers.
Determined to arise from every fall.
Self-made. Transformative. Crossing bridges and
barriers.
Not too stocky to run marathons twice,
A tribute to my brother, a tribute to my wife.

Giving shrewd advice, inspiring completion,
deferring credit to colleagues.
Shunning regret, I resolve unashamedly
To be guided by instinct.
Nearby extended family members make use of my
presence.

My childhood dream of driving my own car
remains a reality.

Uninterrupted I read, write, listen, welcome love.

I work out, cook and eat fish from the oceans where
I once angled.
I did my best at work, helping others promote
human welfare.
After too many tries, I found the love of my life
And we are self-supporting.

In my eighties
In good health, in good spirits,
I continue to defy the expectations of others, which
for me
Are diminished by some
Who disregard me as quiet and likeable.

Laden with stories and observations,
I shape my choices
Do what I please.
My good fortune is like a storied Chanukah candle
A mystical symbol of a miraculous extension.
Death is
Not comprehensible

Aries Zodiac Highlight

Burning

Harper Wells

In a chamber where echoes collide,
Each heartbeat a whisper, a truth I can't hide.
Walls close in, painted with regret,
A dance of despair I cannot forget.

Time stretches thin, an elastic thread,
Moments replay, the living and dead.
Faces flicker like candles in gloom,
Each memory stirs up the weight of the room.

Forever I wander, on paths made of thorns,
In a tapestry woven with feelings of scorn.
Yet within this abyss, a flicker remains,
A whisper of light that quietly wanes.

Caught in this spiral, where pain finds its home,
An odyssey endless, no solace to roam.
Yet even in darkness, the heart beats a plea,
For a moment of stillness, for a chance to be free.

Almost

Megan Wildhood

It's not like I died. And it's not like I'm the one who messed up and almost killed someone. So why am I struggling to live with myself? Ever since my second surgery for appendicitis, I haven't felt like myself. Surely, if I rewind the ribbon of the time tape, I can make everything go differently; I know exactly where everything went wrong, so I know the moment to go back. I've watched the time-travel movies: I know better than to touch anything. All I would have to do is give a different answer to the first question the hospital asked me than the one I actually gave...

"Would you like to participate in this research study?"

Who are you is not coming out of my mouth. It's like my mouth doesn't believe my brain is really commanding it to ask that. It also doesn't believe I want to ask *what research study?*

"Would I get to leave the hospital sooner?" It doesn't sound like my voice, but the young woman with the clipboard at the end of my very long bed nods and smiles like nothing's wrong. "Today!"

There's something wrong.

Yes, I have appendicitis. And no health insurance because I just moved back to Washington and started my new job five days ago.

There's something wrong with the study.

I'm a good person. I want to help people. I *need* to contribute *something* to this life.

There's something wrong.

I might get to avoid surgery altogether. Surgery is to be avoided at most costs, I would think.

There's something wrong.

I would get to avoid surgery and the bill of an overnight stay in the hospital *and* help advance science all at once—I hear "yes, I'll do it" come slooping out of my mouth.

I'm not sure how much time passes after the research study person leaves and someone in scrubs who says she's a surgeon comes in.

"All right, Miss, uh…" she raises just her eyes.

"Wildhood." I keep the *for now* part in my face. I haven't decide whether or not I'll keep that name if divorce is what my husband decides, but it's not his name anyway. Well, it is in that we both changed to a new one, but I was the one who got the name in a dream, and he was the one who took three months to decide to both change and then never actually did change it with the social security office, causing a big problem every year when it comes time to file taxes.

"Right. So, uh…discharging, then?"

"Like, bodily fluid discharge?" I feel the feeling I get when I'm laughing, so I guess that's what happening.

"Got your sense of humor back already," the surgeon snorts. "That's a good sign." She sighs as she scribbles what seems like a whole lot of stuff onto her notepad. "Pharmacy's on the first floor."

She rips off a piece of paper too large to be a prescription, hands it to me, and pats my shoulder. "Good luck! We'll be interested to see how you fare."

Was that an evil glint in her eye?

I realize I can't really trust my own eyes when I look down at the sheet she had just handed me and all I see is snaky, swimmy, tadpoley things shimmying around on it. And off of it onto me— my hand jerks "away" from the paper except that it's the hand holding the paper so the swimmy things come with. Maybe I *do* need this much medication.

Somewhere along the line, I text the friend who had at one point before my marriage—the one that's crumbling but never felt real in the first place anyway—been more than a friend because I'm standing in line at the pharmacy waiting to check out with my drugs when I get a *be there soon* reply text from him. I hadn't bothered to tell my almost ex, probably because our third separation had started almost six months ago and he showed zero percent urgency in repairing anything about our relationship. It wasn't vengeance, it was self-protection: I was tired of feeling like a gnat every time I asked for basic stuff from my husband.

My friend comes and takes me home. He makes sure I had water and emotional support. I fell asleep. I wake up a fuzzy number of time units later to drink some water with my antibiotic pills, which I was to take a ten-day course of instead of surgery so that this research study I had apparently enrolled in soon after they had given me my first-ever dose of Dilaudid and fall back asleep. I wash, rinse, repeat this maybe three more times throughout the night/next day, dragging myself out of bed only to get water and use the bathroom, before the water started tasting like rancid rat carcass. I spit the mouthful out in the tub and crawled on the cool floor, which felt good on the bruises I had gotten from crawling on the floor so much, back to bed. Laying down that time provokes a sense of falling that is equal parts frightening and fun; I awake and fall asleep without disrupting this feeling so many times that, at some point, it starts to feel like falling is the only thing there's ever been.

I wake up and sleep, wake up and sleep, wake up and sleep, wake, sleep, wake, sleep I lose track of how many times before I jolt awake by being shot at point-blank range. From the inside. I can barely crawl to the bathroom in time to try to vomit. It hurts too much to complete the heave. I lie down on the cold tile, pressing my abdomen into the soothing chill as hard as I could stand it until the friend who I had made plans with for dinner was gently but rapidly tapping my shoulder blade. One of my eight housemates must have let her in despite none of them coming to check on me. Just as well – I didn't know any of their names and the only time I'd ever spoken to one of them was to ask where my entire grocery order had gone after I'd put it in the fridge less than an hour before. The answer was as Seattle as that living situation: wordless shrug, no eye contact, accidental arm bump as she passed me back to her dank hovel of a bedroom.

"I'm so sorry!" The words are slurred coming out but sincere. I *always* do what I say and I always keep my commitments, even when I make too many and most of them I make because I think it will make me worthy of friendship rather than out of any actual desire to do so. "We're supposed to have di—"

"I'm taking you to the ER," she says in her signature firmkindconfidentcaring voice.

I shake my head vigorously enough to hear bones sliding around on each other in my neck.

"Why won't you go when you feel this bad?" She kneels next to me.

"Because they'll admit me. Plus," I pause to catch my breath after struggling and failing to sit up, "the nurse said this was just a symptom of peritonitis." I struggle again to sit up, this time succeeding only with the help of the cabinet.

"When did you call the nurse? Did you tell her what your pain level is?" She stands up and reaches out her hand. Before I can answer, she frowns. "I thought you had appendicitis."

Apparently, whatever I said next doesn't make sense because her face drains of color and she calls for help getting me into her car.

The next thing I remember is my almost-ex-husband finally coming to visit, but this may have happened the day they discharged me. We weren't talking every day at that point, but I remember thinking he should know about this. Maybe I was hoping it would spur him to pursue relationship with me, just like every other emergency, which had inspired acute care and concern from him for a few months tops each time.

What it inspired, whenever it happened, was indeed a visit—and a gift: a purplish, viney plant, which, I have to hand it to him, is very me in many ways. There isn't much dialogue between us, I'm sure, and the second surgery I would need to finally remove my appendix would sort of hork my memory out of whack, so I wouldn't remember it anyway by now. It still is the last time, as of this writing, that I've seen him, as I knew then that it would be, even as it would take another 11 months for the paperwork to finalize our divorce to go through.

Just as I knew in my knower that I should have just done the surgery. I should not have consented to being in a research study, not least because there is no follow up at all when you report negative outcomes. But also because, had I not just asked them the day my coworker drove me to the hospital to perform the appendectomy, I might not have needed the second surgery, which they had to do because the first time they tried to evict my appendix, they couldn't find it, everything was too swollen and infected; all they could do was drain the abscess that had formed (that was the being-shot-level pain) and a pound of necrotic tissue without risking hemorrhage. I might have been able to avoid two doses of general anesthesia too close together and save my brain. I might still be able to find words lightning fast, remember everything I hear, not take months instead of hours to write anything.

But also, I might not ever have met my fiancé Sam, the absolute best thing that God has given to me and I would not have ever experienced being truly loved and cared for in the self-sacrificial way my first husband wasn't mature enough to handle when he was compelled to propose to me after five years of rough on/off relationship, if I had answered the question the hospital asked me this way instead:

"Would you like to participate in this research study?" A woman with mean-girl cheekbones and an expression to match holds an iPad or two or several in front of my face. Normally, I'm someone who likes a lot of information—learning that this is more FOMO than merely striving to stay informed—and it sure seems like I've missed a big chunk of it here.

But is this really the time? One of my organ's tried to kill me. Take it out.

But....surgery. *Surgery.* I'm essentially alone. I'm only married on paper and none of my family is in state, which was the point, but that's another story.

Take it out.

The last two times I have ignored this gut feeling/intuition/whisper from the Holy Spirit did not go well, though one of them could *maybe* still work out. I shouldn't have married the guy I married, but we've hung on through two other separations. Maybe a medical crisis is just the jolt he needs to prioritize our healing.

I can't say *no.* This is science or something! It's for the good of humanity. Or at least me, who gets to avoid the horrific welter of guilt that comes with having to say no in order to take care of myself, god forbid just because I *don't want* to meet a request.

There's something wrong.

Yes, I have appendicitis. And no health insurance because I just moved back to Washington after trying to escape my crumbling nothing of a marriage and started my new job five days ago so am having to take unpaid leave as well.

There's something wrong. Take it out.

I'm a good person. I want to help people. I *need* to contribute *something* to this life.

There's something wrong. Take it out.

I swallow. "I think I'd rather," I take a breath in attempts to stabilize the room that has started to wobble, "Yeah, I think I'd rather just get my appendix removed." I choke on the wave of nausea that arises from failing to people please, which I try to tell myself is because of the painkillers they shot me full of as soon as they started the CT to confirm appendicitis.

"Oooookay," is all iPad lady says before she stands and leaves.

It is definitely at least a half hour before a horde of medical people come in, all moving as one and saying nothing that makes any sense until they ask me who my emergency contact is. It seems like they say it at least twice because they're kind of impatient after a while. But I'm still deciding—I moved away from Washington because I no longer had community and didn't want to go through a divorce alone, if that's what was going to happen, and my family is 1,300 miles away. The only person who's close to nearby who might respond—has responded to emergencies (and really only emergencies) in the past—is my maybe almost ex. I have to say my ex.

He comes. It's a long while later I think, but he has a plant! Potted because he remembers that cut flowers make me sad; you're just watching them die slowly in the vase. We don't say much, but do we really need to? Maybe my "need" for verbal engagement is more of a compulsion to avoid silence. Maybe I can be okay with quiet.

They wheel me back for surgery and I imagine it's just like the movies. What if it could be that dramatic? Doctors' brows furrowed, nurse staff rushing, onlookers praying, minor chords clanging, as my gurney squeals through angel-white hallways until severe watertight doors slam behind me and the team that will save my life.

But it's a quiet event: I'm in the room I was admitted to with my maybe-not-almost-ex. Then, I'm in prep. Then, I'm in the OR, counting backwards from 100 while fog fingers in from my periphery, as thick as forever.

The procedure is over in the blink of an eye and I return to myself extra quick—my body processes anesthesia surprisingly efficiently, apparently. My not-yet-ex has just arrived again after going back to work for the two hours that my surgery actually lasted; I don't yet know the pain from the former will be chronic, but I don't think I'll be surprised when I learn that it is: the pain from the latter is almost something I can get used to, maybe with just a few more decades. *Almost.*

Maybe it's my fuzzy mind and pain-fatigued soul speaking here, but I think I really mean it when I say: thank God it went the former way and not the latter.

March New Moon Special

Care

Avery Walker

Hearts beat loud, yet hollow,
In the midst of the masquerade.
I watch the dance, the vibrant swirl,
But find no warmth in any twirl.

The whispers of worry, the cries of despair,
Yet here I sit, with a heart made of stone,
"Do you not care?" they question with frowns,
As I wander through their ups and downs.

Compassion's a burden, a weight to be burned.
For in caring, there's a chaos of pain and disdain.
So let them weep over their human affair,
For I've learned that it's easier to simply not care.

Living Elegy

Wyatt Strawbridge

Clean, pristine, palace,
Worship yourself, Anno domini stops
At 2005, and I've never been
More delighted to laud the new lord,
Built brick by brick, a labor of love past
The initial labor, proud future thee should be,
I'll celebrate and see the masses mag
'Proud *pueri*, proudly *sequitur ventrem*'
And let me, your humble devote, be
A stone, or more of years in the life,
To stand on solidly.

Hung Up in a Gibbet

Michael Roque

Locked—
Hanging in a gibbet—
suspended on outskirts

a daydreamer
existing between laughs, chatter heard,
sweat-stung blisters felt—
hurt—

dreams caged in gibbet—
of feet on earth

to meet the them below,
see eye to eye,
take into soul what makes cities stir—

Delirium
engulfed gibbet—
diminishing—
unalert

parched, pleading to be freed—
tucked in the hung's pocket
the gibbet's key—
rebirth.

April Full Moon Special

Catastrophe

Samuel Brown

In the silent hours before dawn,
the moon hung heavy, unblinking, a silent sentinel
in the cold black sky.
Its once gentle glow had grown jagged, fractured,
like shards of ice caught in a celestial storm.

Then, a tremor—an unseen shiver—coursed
through the cosmos,
a whisper of chaos stirring behind the velvet curtain
of night.
Slowly, inexorably, the moon veered from its calm
path,
its face twisted in a silent scream, a silent warning
no one heard.

Time seemed to stretch and fracture as the great orb
began its descent,
a terrible, relentless plummet toward the trembling
earth below.
Stars flickered in fear, their flickering dimmed as
the sky darkened further,
a shadow swallowing the universe's last remnants
of light.

The ground shuddered beneath our feet—trees
bending, buildings creaking—
as the moon drew closer, a dark monolith of
ancient, unyielding stone,
crashing through clouds like a demon breaking free
from its cage,
its surface scarred with the scars of cosmic
violence.

Cracks formed in the earth, fissures yawning wide,
devouring everything in their path—cities, forests,
memories—
each rupture a wound in the world, bleeding chaos
into the veins of the land.

A deafening roar, not quite sound but a wave of
dread,
ripped through the air as the moon collided,
a collision of silence and fury,
shattering the horizon into shards of nightmare.

In the fallout of that celestial fury,
the sky itself seemed to bleed—a scar across the
heavens—
and beneath, the earth was forever altered,
a landscape haunted by the ghost of what once was,
a warning whispered in the dark:
some things in the universe are not meant to be
disturbed.

Reflection Prisoner

Wyatt Strawbridge

In a prison lie, don't die, to the guards,
The mind. Stoke the heart's fire, search
Inquire, from all God's choir, where and when
You went wrong, let your contrition be a song
On fair, sweet spring air, that'll go
Tell it on the mountain how, there's quiet power
In this early hour, where soft voices grow
Proud, control their range, and show,
How from their licking, their nappy mother tongue,
Natural birth, and understanding of dearth,
Were shaped from whelp to man.
Pick and eat apples galore, then pore
Out, sated, gospel and gossip, be both,
Divine trinity within me, let me,
Pledge myself: an imperfect, forgiven, devotee
Of that glorious garden and my wise words.

Infinity Hides in Your Mind

Michael Roque

We all know what a mind is made of—
our own,
but if I could crawl between the crevices of your
brain,
get lost in a thought—
maybe see the whole production line,
would I find something familiar?
Something like mine?
The morbid, the cruel,
or would I meet something sweet, innocent,
wholesome—
A beauty—
so long gone for me.

What drifts in your infinite universe?
What thoughts are echoing over what backdrops?
What rushes at you from the dark alleyway you
move toward,
when your head's on the pillow at 10 p.m.?

The meteorites you throw at me are nice—
but I want your whole asteroid to pulverize
the face of my planet.
I want to be shaken by your advancing booms,
burnt by the fire,
rearranged by the underworld
you feel you need to hide.

Taurus Zodiac Highlight

Steadfast

Finley Parker

In quiet strength, the steady hand prevails, a beacon
shining through the storm's harsh might,
unwavering when others falter or fail, their steadfast
heart remains a guiding light.

With patience as their silent, enduring song, they
wait with grace through tempests and despair,
knowing that hope endures, though it be long, in
time, the fruits of labor will be there.

Practical minds that see through fleeting haze, they
build with purpose, grounded, clear, and true,
transforming dreams into tangible days, their work
reflects a vision fresh and new.

Loyal souls who stand through thick and thin,
persistent in pursuit of what is right, their
dedication deep, from deep within, they chase their
goals with relentless might.

Diligent hearts that never cease in strive,
endeavoring past fatigue and doubt, their resolve
keeps dreams and hopes alive, a testament to what
true strength's about.

Thus, in their steadfast, patient, practical way, lies a
power that can shape the world anew, for those who
work with loyalty each day, create a legacy both
brave and true.

The Interrogation

Douglas Young

Deputy Sheriff Freddy McTavis eased his large waistline into his chair to face the nervous man and his attorney across the interrogation room table. Deputy McTavis had never liked the well-tailored gentleman he brought in for questioning, recalling all the times he saw handsome Gram Tanner cut up in school and never get in trouble. Instead, teachers thought he was cute and ever so witty. Freddy never found his jokes funny, but the one time he remembered himself joking during class, he got sent to detention.

Unlike short and pudgy Freddy, who failed to make their high school football team, tall and lean Gram became the star quarterback dating the prettiest girls. While Freddy obeyed every school rule, he saw classmates slip Gram cheat sheets during tests, and he knew Gram smoked marijuana under the school bleachers. Unlike many others, Mr. Tanner never got caught.

After graduation, Gram went to an out-of-state university where he got a business degree and was his fraternity's president. He returned home to become vice president at his father's factory where Freddy's mother still worked as a cleaning lady. Gram married his prom queen sweetheart, had three beautiful children, bought a large home in the town's most exclusive gated neighborhood, became a deacon in its biggest Baptist church, and was now rumored to be mulling a run for city council. Freddy also heard that Gram's dad needed the council to approve his zoning request to build another factory.

Meanwhile Freddy began working for the local sheriff's department right after high school. His job dominated his life. While occasionally disgusted with some of the people it forced him to deal with, the work gave him far more purpose and respect than he had ever known, though he knew some locals laughed at his girth. But he enjoyed helping people and, by age thirty, had saved enough money to move out of his mother's apartment into his own trailer behind the railroad tracks on the edge of town. Never comfortable dating, he socialized with brother deputies at diners and fast-food eateries, as well as over weekend beers, cook-outs, movies, and videogames at the homes of the dwindling number still single.

When Janiyah Sims was reported missing, Deputy McTavis was assigned the case and soon learned that Janiyah's mother was Gram's family's maid. The girl's friends also claimed to have frequently seen the nineteen-year-old in the same car with thirty-five-year-old Gram Tanner.

Because Gram neither answered nor returned his calls, Deputy McTavis had rung the Tanner doorbell around 6 p.m. to ask an alarmed Mrs. Jenny Tanner in her kitchen apron if he could please speak with her husband.

"What's this about, Freddy?"

"Well, Miss Jenny, y'all's maid's daughter, Janiyah, has gone missing—"

"Oh, my Lord!"

"And folks say they've recently seen her riding with Gram. Does he still drive that blue BMW sports car?"

"Yes," she answered softly looking away. The young Tanner children now huddled around their white-faced mother.

"Y'all go back to the living room and watch TV," she ordered in a loud voice as a blinking Gram Tanner came to the front door.

"Hey, Gram. Say, why don't we go downtown," Freddy suggested. "I don't want to disrupt things anymore here at home,"

"Are you taking my Daddy to jail?" the four-year-old girl asked.

"No, darling," Deputy McTavis said kneeling. "Daddy ain't being arrested. He's just gon' help the police find somebody."

"Honey, what's going on?" Jenny asked her husband.

"I don't know, babe," he replied. "Just call Jack Cheatem, the family lawyer, and tell him to meet me at the sheriff's department."

Sitting in an interrogation room, Freddy McTavis faced a far more-quiet and hunched-over Gram Tanner than he had ever seen. His hair was somewhat disheveled, his hands were clasped against his mouth as if praying, and his eyes seemed unfocused. His attorney stared at the deputy.

"Gram," Freddy began, "I 'preciate you coming down here. I figured it might be best if we didn't talk in front of Miss Jenny and the young'uns."

Mr. Cheatem turned to see his client nod and mouth "Thank you."

"I'm 'fraid we've got ourselves a missing gal, Miss Janiyah Sims," Deputy McTavish continued. "Now a mess of witnesses claim they've recently seen her in your car with you at the wheel throughout Raleigh Colston County. So I gotta' ask if you know where Miss Janiyah might be and, if you don't, then when and where did you last see or have contact with her, what's the nature of y'all's relationship—"

"Any charges against my client?" Jack Cheatem interrupted loudly.

Deputy McTavis blinked and jumped slightly. He always tried hard to set just the right mood to induce persons of interest to confess or offer good information.

"'Cause, unless you have any, we're done here, Barney Fife. Come on, Gram." Jack jumped up and motioned for his client to join him.

"You don't want to help find a missing girl?" the deputy asked Gram. "Sheriff Moody and the D.A.'ll be here any minute—"

"Good. Y'all have a real fine circle jerk." The attorney declared as he steered his client toward the door.

"This could be a deadly serious matter, Gram," a now standing Deputy McTavis declared.

"Y'all just have a big time." Jack grinned. "Hey, maybe they'll let you pitch this time."

Gram avoided Freddy's face as he followed his lawyer out the door. In the parking lot he turned to him.

"What gives, Jack? I can't believe you talked to him like that, a deputy sheriff and a classmate of mine."

"Richly deserved -- every damn word. Assholes intimidating my clients need to hear the unvarnished truth."

Freddy McTavis slowly gathered his notes, figuring the star athlete son of his mother's boss would likely skate over whatever he may have done, just like in school.

Deputy Jethro Simpson opened the door. "Freddy, Willie's still out sick and I gotta' go on patrol. So the sheriff says somebody's gotta' clean up the men's room."

Another Natural Disaster

Michael Roque

Soft tones, stray stares
stacked upon another day—
add pressure to a boiling core,
coercing shifts and movements,
bringing tectonic plates to crash—
Causing quakes—
tumbling cityscapes we'd just begun building,
cracking sidewalks and roads we mock-paved.

When two winds fail to follow a united flow
across shared skies,
and opt to entwine
over moving beautifully—
rhythmically—
side by side,
town meets tornado—
trees uproot, structures fold,
more innocence dies.
between two well-meaning souls.

A long list of natural disasters
hang under my name
from the years of yous—
from facing down pressures—
too high to hide.

April New Moon Special

Goddess Ambrosial

Kaylyn Dunn

The night would be lost
Without her ever present radiance
The bright glow of her hair
Could not lead the stars
The pale porcelain of her skin
Could not light the dark
She goes by many names
But to each she does not answer
Instead she sits confined to the clouds
And hidden behind the wind

White

Luke Reuteman

She began to unwrap the white offering,
A butcher's paper package with red string bow.
Delicately peeling back the tape, she revealed
A quaint box of thick-cut bacon,
A tube of her favorite Christmas sausage,
A wedge of cheese, a loaf of bread, and a half-dozen
eggs.
He smiled sweetly to her when she looked.

As she turned for him to kiss her cheek,
She gazed out to the dusty white behind him
Streaming down from the black roof
Then eddying high in the breezeway alcove.
It was lovely, the sheer drapes it slung,
Billowing open to the neighborhood.
But the snow was drift not freshly falling, and soon,
Once the gusts tired out,
Settled again onto the crusted pavement
Like a snow globe's glitter
Atop painted families.

She breathed deeply as she stood,
Wincing in her eyes at the top
When her inky ribs jabbed back,
And slid the cast iron onto the front burner.
She lit a match and turned the left knob
To start on his breakfast,
But she waited too long
To touch the match
To the burner,
So there was a loud
whoomp
When she did.

Civilization On a Block of Ice

Michael Roque

Life—
on solid plateaus
of outstretched ice.
Serene to ears
sanctuary space for penguins, seals,
shady place for circling aquatics seaside.

Warm glimmer,
a nice tan,
a random morning sunrise,
morphed into blinding shine,
Sweat beads piling on penguins' brows.
Dehydration sets into delirium pleas
from parched mouths

Our wide expanse of ice
Shrink, shrinks-
Finally sinks.
Waters boil,
waters rise,
submerging into memories,
the bars, the shows, the old skyline.

Now—
an ecosystem sits
on a melting cube of ice
waiting for settling tides,

for the sun to set for a cold winter
to rain hail upon smoldering life.

May Full Moon Special

We are the motherline

Alison Brechtel

A circle of women surrounds me.
That circle blesses me.
And roots me on from afar.
They are the watchers.
I am the doer.

They give me life.
And place their hands on my belly.

I can see them in Emmy's big brown eyes, when
she smiles and they crinkle.
In her laugh that travels up and down and down
and up.
They are rooting her on.
They place their hands in the air, aiming her to
walk in their direction.
They are clapping when she claps.

I can see my gram behind my mom.
She's placing my hand on her shoulder.
Just as my mom places a hand on mine.

I can see the line
I can see the line so clearly
Of my grandmother, my mom, myself, and
Emmy.
We are the evolution.
Evolution of the beauty.
And evolution of the mess.
Evolution of the chaos in the world and us.

Together, we are one
We are the motherline.

Prequel to a Mount

Luke Reuteman

A doe contours a timber ridge
Between her meal and bed,
Her body changing like the leaves
From green to fiery red.

A buck on southern slope to sun
Sticks nose into the breeze,
Inhaling newfound heaviness
And musk among the trees.

Arising off the ground he feels
his senses start to slur
from sunning, now, to tunneled thoughts
of sudden lust for her.

Through swarms of autumn olive thorns
And mats of acorn caps,
He travels well-known highway roads
Not shown on local maps

'Til finally, crescendoed scent
Reveals her amongst the hay.
The gap is closed, and doe and buck
May now commence their play.

She canters off, he gives her chase,
They circle 'round the trees,
And do this several times respecting
Old formalities.

His crown stands tall upon his brow,

Though chipped from proving clout;
Their young will likely grow as strong,
No need to draw this out.

He marches up, aflame in mind—
Her ears give sudden flick;
She wonders if her lover heard
That faint, metallic click.

When Life Gives You Lemons

Taliesin Gore

Coming home to an empty apartment
slick with the sweat of other men's affairs,
he sinks into his old leather sofa;
sighs as he pulls a tube of lipstick from
the crease between the cushions; wearily
surveys the kingdom of his desolation,
no longer even monarch of his home.
The man and the apartment seem to have grown
into each other in a symbiosis
of mutual decay. Until, at last,
brain reeling with exhaustion, images
of everything he's seen that day, like in
the movies, he nods his head and goes to sleep.
Waking up in an empty apartment,
littered with the paraphernalia
of conquests not his own, he groggily
peels himself off the sofa, rubs his face,
and looks around him with a doleful air.
He sleepwalks to the bathroom, shaves, cuts
himself in various places and applies
shreds of tissue, stuck on with spots of blood.
Then for a while he gazes at his face:
a constellation of red dots upon
the faded map of an undistinguished life,
drawn on by dime-store dreams. And on and on
he goes about the business of preparing
himself to face another same-old day.
You might think he'd resent this halfway life,
a kind of hotel steward of his home,
only inhabiting the spaces left
by other men who use him to their ends.

But Mr. Lemon doesn't have sour grapes.
He's an eternal optimist, poor soul.
He goes to work in the metropolis.
He's kind of a professional third wheel.
He flicks his fingers through the paper wheel
of names and numbers standing on his desk,
and makes arrangements for his clientele:
the men above him in the corporate ladder.
One of these days they'll throw a dog a bone.
Or at least they keep saying that they will.
And that's enough for Mr. Lemon. See,
Mr. Lemon's the kind of guy who lives
in constant hope of something wonderful
descending on him from the universe.
He sits there in his cramped cubicle;
chatters like a monkey on the phone;
presses a desultory finger on
the typewriter every now and again.
The guy he works for is a total heel,
a thrusting businessman, an alpha male.
And back in the apartment, after hours,
he's one of Mr. Lemon's regulars.
There's this girl he's been seeing for a while,
keeps telling her he's gonna leave his wife
but somehow never does. You know the deal.
Now Mr. Lemon wouldn't treat a girl
like that, you know? 'Cos he's the real deal.
'Cos Mr. Lemon, he's a real nice guy,
the kind you might take home to show your folks.
The kind who likes his eggs sunny side up,
and only eats the yolks. An optimist!
And in the mornings and the evenings, when
he rides the rigging of the ship of steel
that crests the wave of cold modernity
(the building where he goes to work each day),

he tries to chat up the elevator girl.
And she's a real peach, ya' know? But she
is real hung up on Mr. Lemon's boss.
That's right. The very same. But he, poor soul,
hasn't made the connection yet. But hell.
We'll let him carry on in ignorance
a little while. Let a dog have his day.
She seems to kinda like his goofy jokes,
puppy-dog eagerness and innocence.
She isn't even creeped out by the fact
he used his private detective skills to track
down her name and address. (Well, I guess
people are a lot less paranoid
during this period of history.)
Of course, she probably sees him more as friend
material, but he can work with that.
She tells him she's about to finish things
with an old fling, an on-and-off affair,
an older man, the kind young women fall for.
It's been going on for months. But now
she knows all this time he's been stringing her
along. Keeps saying he's gonna leave his wife
and run away with her, but somehow, it's
never the right time. You know the way.
And Mr. Lemon nods in sympathy.
Oh yeah. Sure. It's time to cut all ties.
Long overdue. Move on to greener prospects.
Hey, by the way, would you like to see a movie
with me tomorrow night? It's no big deal.
I happened to be going anyway,
thought maybe you could use the company,
considering what you're going through and all.
She smiles: Why sure! I think that would be swell.
So later, when he's riding in the subway,
surrounded by the other human ants,

indifferent businessmen and secretaries,
he starts to entertain a fantasy.
It's pretty much your standard movie fare:
a sunny day, a picnic, him and her,
clinking glasses, leaning close together;
first kiss; wedding ring in a glass of fizz;
delighted squeal; the breathless 'Yes, I will,'
and soon enough (the montage carries on)
a lot of little Lemons running around,
playing, fighting, growing; off to college,
first love, first heartbreak; home for holidays;
the pair of them (Mr. and Mrs Lemon)
growing old and love-worn; grandchildren;
wearing matching knitted hats and jumpers;
standing at a gate to watch the sunset.
You know the drill. The dreams of men are made
in celluloid. Like fragile flowers, at once
authentic and derivative, sincere
and ersatz, they flourish in the cracks that fracture
the concrete pavements of modernity,
yet never threaten its integrity.
So, for a while he wanders around the city,
eats in a half-full diner, where the plates,
the knives and forks, the faded chrome tables
and worn-out faces of the other diners
all glow with a dusky film-projector light,
and seem complicit in his happiness.
And so, as the appointed time approaches,
he leaves and makes his way back through the
streets,
through urban ravines, steep-sided, overshadowed
by the dark shapes of skyscrapers, through
the slums and run-down tenements, and under
the soft, unnatural gloaming of the streetlights.
At last, he reaches the apartment building.

He climbs the stairs and finds himself before
his door. He opens it and peers inside.
and in the apartment there's this strange tableau:
a stage-set for an intimate scene, vacated,
like a discarded wrapper, the actors fled,
perhaps to greener pastures. Table set
for two; empty wine bottle, traces of
red liquid clinging to the insides of
two glasses; dregs like little pools of blood
cradled in the bottoms; and the smell
of something unborn murdered in the womb.
Oh, and one more detail: a little scrap
of paper on the table, blotted with blood-
red drops of wine, the masculine hand-writing:
I've done it. Left my wife. So what d'you say?
Beneath, the one line in a girlish hand,
a little shaky with emotion, Yes,
I will. And last of all, the final piece:
he sees the imprint of the wedding ring,
limned faintly in a wash of half-dried wine.
He stands there a moment, dumbstruck, numb, a
sleep-
walker slowly awaking from a dream.
He's kind of like that cartoon coyote who
keeps on running in mid-air until
he looks down, realizes that the ground's
vanished from under him, and even then
pauses to register his situation
before he finally begins to fall,
leaving nothing but a puff of smoke.
Just so the ground beneath him falls away:
from walking on air to freefall in a delayed
split second. This is the way reality
kicks in, the way he finally correlates
the contents of his mind. Maybe you think

this is a pretty big leap to make, that one
of such an optimistic cast of mind
as Mr. Lemon would most likely lack
the means to draw the invisible lines connecting
this constellation of dots, like blood-red stars
in a sky become suddenly baleful, alien.
And surely such an intuition for
disaster would much more befit a man
with the perceptive apparatus of
a pessimist. You'd probably be right.
Maybe you think this whole scene's contrived,
and lacking the objective correlative
to justify this sudden revelation.
You're probably right there too. The truth is, I'm
no Mr. Lemon, nor a Mr Wilder
for that matter. No, I'm a dyed-in-the-wool
pessimist, a glass-half-empty kind
of guy. You know the type. And, well, I just
can't bring myself to give a character
a happy ending. It offends my sense
of truth. But still, I'd have you understand
that Mr. Lemon is my shadow and
perhaps I'm his; and that this gives us a
particular connection to each other;
that each, perhaps, in his intensest moments,
pierces the veil of his reality
and glimpses the other's inverted world, and maybe
that world invades his own. For I believe
that opposites contain each other's seeds:
Carl Jung called this "enantiodromia."
So now I've got that apologia
out of the way, back to Mr. Lemon.
He has his revelation (regardless of whether
you think it's believable or not),
and as the sense of gravity starts to sink

into his dazed brain, he begins to reel,
walks slowly to the cabinet, gets out
a bottle of whisky, half empty, downs it all
in one long draught, determined to drown the whole
world beneath a sea of alcohol.
This done, he staggers out the door and down
the stairs and into the nightmare of the night.
He finds his way into the city centre,
illumined store-fronts looming luridly
over him, and tower-blocks ascending
like impossible monoliths against
the starless half-light of the civic sky,
its opalescent light-polluted mist.
At last, he winds up in some seedy bar.
And on the stage, a seedy singer's singing
maudlin melodies that linger on
his tongue with a horrible, cold irony,
a coppery aftertaste, a tang of rust.
Listening, he orders drink after drink,
blearily looks about him with a faint
light of accusation in his eyes,
as if the place's patrons are all a part
of some conspiracy against him. Really,
nobody takes much notice of him. He
doesn't look out of place in a place like this:
another hulk among the derelicts,
another piece of human set-dressing,
slowly sinking into the scenery,
a bit part in the movie of his life.
All his time he dreamed he was the hero,
and now he wakes to find himself alone,
the moonlight of his life-illusion waning,
another lonely no one in the crowd,
another life of quiet desperation.
He sits and drinks his bitterness to the dregs.

Then, mumbling to himself, he drags himself
back out into the street, and finds his feet
mechanically remembering the way,
and after a blurry, liquor-slurred passage of time
finds himself suddenly back in his apartment.
And in the apartment there's that awful smell
of stale champagne and other men's amours.
He stumbles about the apartment for a while,
then tumbles into bed and restless sleep.
And Mr. Lemon dreams of a great wheel.
He's in some TV game show. There's the girl,
playing the beautiful assistant in
the game show of his dream. Our Lady Fortune.
And he, himself, spread-eagled on the wheel,
nails in his palms and feet, like Leonardo's
Vitruvian man (but thinning on the top
and slightly stooped). And then the game-show
host's
stentorian voice is reading out his fate:
Ooh. Tough luck, Mr. Lemon. Looks like you're
going home empty handed on this occasion.
And the invisible audience says Awww
as the dream spins out of focus, fades to black.
Waking up in an empty apartment,
surrounded by the wreckage of his life,
a pounding redness in his head, he drags
himself out of bed and into the bathroom,
looks at the razor on the washstand, and
looks at the razor on the washstand for
a dramatically long moment, and
picks up the tin of shaving cream beside it.
Maybe he'll catch that movie after all.

* *This poem is a reimagining of Billy Wilder's 1960
film* The Apartment.

Gemini Zodiac Highlight

Shards

Emma Kim

In the quiet hours when the night breathes shallow,
I feel the shifting sands beneath my skin,
A thousand whispers flickering like candle
flames—
Flickering but never steady, never still.

I am the mirror cracked in two,
Reflections splintered across fractured surfaces,
Each fragment holding a different truth,
A different face I wear in different worlds,
Never quite the same, never quite enough.

My thoughts dart like shadows—
silent, fleeting, impossible to grasp,
A dance of duality, a constant tug between
what is and what could be,
what I show and what I hide.

I sense the unseen currents pulling at my edges,
A whisper of night, a breath of dawn,
A voice that is not mine but calls within—
asking, questioning, demanding to be heard,
yet never revealing itself fully.

Sometimes I feel the weight of a thousand selves,
pressing inward, pressing outward—
a pressure that cracks open the mind,
letting in glimpses of chaos lurking just beneath
the surface of my calm exterior.

I walk the line between worlds,
hovering on the edge of what's known and
unknown,
each step a delicate balance,
each move a secret choreography,
danced in the dark, unseen but felt.

The air around me hums softly with muted alarms,
a lullaby woven from shadows and whispers,
telling tales of things I dare not understand,
things lurking just beyond the veil of perception—
waiting, watching, whispering my name in the dark.

And in those moments of quiet,
when the world grows still and the stars seem to
pulse with secrets,
I wonder—am I the keeper of these whispers,
or merely a vessel for the chaos they bring?
A fragment caught between the flickering lights
of a thousand shifting selves,
lost somewhere in the endless dance of shadows.

The Doubler

Luke Reuteman

On a whim, he bought four chicks,
Spent too much on coop and feeds,
And gave them names, as if they cared,
Of Fancy, Flirty, Frisky, Phoebes.
They stunk the house and spare room bed
'Til outside they could finally sleep,
Where raccoons dug into the coop
And picked out two for them to eat.
Two chickens hardly make a farm--
A Craigslist granny gave four, free.
And over hens that would soon kill
Their kin, she'd tear up motherly.
Yes, five of them would corner one
And dip their beaks in cherry tea,
And drunk one eve, he'd not closed coop
So coons, another, would head-be.
All still without the maiden egg
The cast had been half-bagged debris,
But when the first egg was a doubler,
He figured it was meant to be.

Ruth

Taliesin Gore

In freshers' week, we had a party in
our flat. That's where I met her. Her gay
friend introduced us: a tall guy,
good-looking, with almond eyes and olive skin.
He asked me if I thought she was pretty
and I assented with a sheepish grin.
We flirted awkwardly throughout the party,
then she invited me back to her flat for coffee.
It was just down the road. We sat at the kitchen
table for a while, talking awkwardly
about our creative ambitions: mine was poetry,

hers acting. I told her my favourite poet was Keats,
and 'Ode to a Nightingale' my favourite poem.
She remembered it because of her namesake's
cameo. At some point she took her barrettes
out of her hair and put them on the table; and at
some
point I absent-mindedly picked one up
and started fiddling with the metal clip.

The whole time I was kicking myself inside.
I knew I ought to make some kind of move.
I just couldn't take the initiative. In the end
she ran out of patience and told me to leave.
'And I'll have that back,' she snapped, snatching
the hairpin
out of my hand, and ferried me outside.
I was almost out the front door of the building when
I checked my jacket pocket and couldn't find
my phone. I turned,

went all the way back up the three or four
flights of stairs and timidly tapped on her door.
I waited, searched myself again, found
it, hesitated for a moment, turned
and hurried back down the stairs. Half way down
I thought I heard her door open. But by then
my courage was spent and it was too late to turn

back. We spoke on one other occasion,
and I saw her around every now and then.
Then, one day, I think it was in third year,
Facebook informed me she was In a Relationship.
And there was a picture of the happy pair:
a guy with thick-rimmed glasses, long black hair;
him grinning, her glowing with possessive love.
They looked a regular pair of turtle doves.

But I think he must've given her the slip.
A few months later I saw her outside the library,
sitting on a bench, against the glass partition,
bent over, sobbing into her hands. I felt vaguely
guilty, not only for my inaction then,
but somehow complicit through our shared history,
as glancing as that history had been.

And now, looking back from this vantage of time,
this ridiculous daisy chain
of egocentric reasoning conspires
to place the blame of her sorrow on my shoulders.
Perhaps, I think, the prophecy of her name
had come to cruel fruition;
that conversation in her kitchen was
the invocation of some Keatsian curse;
and my inaction at the fateful moment

set into motion a baleful chain of events
that left her on that bench, forlorn,
'in tears amid the alien corn.'

May New Moon Special

Held

Huina Zheng

The usually bustling brick factory had quieted on the twenty-eighth day of the twelfth lunar month, as the workers left for their Spring Festival break. Ling didn't care how they planned to prepare for or spend the holiday. Six days weren't enough to return all the way to Sichuan, and most of the factory's forty-some married men had left their wives and children back home. The burden of holiday preparations belonged to the women. She felt no envy as the men napped, played cards, or wandered the nearby markets. She had long grown used to it—men resting during holidays while women rushed about, holding everything together.

Under the warm sun, Ling crouched by the courtyard well, scrubbing curtains. The sunlight burned faintly on her back. She wanted to finish while the weather was good, so the pre-festival cleaning could be wrapped up. After that, she still had to pick up the last of the holiday groceries, then snip the cured sausages into pieces and bind them with red thread.

"Get on your knees!"

Yao's roar tore through the air, laced with Ming's pleading and muffled sobs. Ling's heart jolted. Dread surged through her.

She stumbled inside. Ming was kneeling on the bare concrete floor, his small body trembling. At eight years old, his knees were no match for the cold, hard surface. Yao's business partner, Sheng, sat at the tea table. When Ling entered, he looked over, startled and unsure what to do.

"What happened?" she asked, her voice barely audible.

"Your son stole money!" Yao's voice was low and hard, each word ground out between clenched teeth. "This boy—Zhang Yao's son—is a thief. I'm working day and night—no time to discipline him—and this is what he becomes? No upbringing. No respect. What will people think if they hear?"

"There must be a mistake. Ming wouldn't do that." Ling stepped closer to her son. She reached out, then stopped, afraid of provoking Yao. Lowering her voice, she said, "Ming, tell Mama. What happened?"

"Mama, I..." Ming's voice shook. "I... I'll never do it again... I promise..."

"He's eight years old. It's shameful... having him kneel like this..." Ling hated the pleading in her voice, but she only wanted it all to stop. Her eyes flicked to Sheng, silently asking for help.

Sheng set down his gongfu teacup, and with an almost imperceptible nod, stood up and walked over. "Yao, he's still a child. There's time to teach him. It's almost Chinese New Year."

He gently helped Ming up. "Go on back to your room," he said.

Ming glanced at Yao, fear in his eyes. His hands clutched the hem of his shirt, fingers trembling. Ling's heart clenched.

She longed to go over and hold him, but she was afraid Yao would explode again. All she could do was watch as Ming shuffled toward his room, each step tentative. He touched the doorknob so lightly it was as if he feared making a sound. He pushed the door open and went inside. When it closed behind him, Ling thought she could hear him sobbing.

"This is what happens when you spoil him and shield him," Yao shouted, his voice echoing through the courtyard. "He ends up stealing! I work myself to the bone at the brick factory. I'd give my life for this family! And what do you do? You pamper him all day long. Indulgence ruins a child—haven't you heard that? And still you keep coddling him!"

More workers gathered outside. They craned their necks, peering into the house, whispering in Sichuanese. It was close enough to Mandarin that Ling could understand. Some said she was pitiful— that no woman should be humiliated like this in front of so many. Others said Yao was right to scold his wife—what was wrong with that?

Ling lowered her head until her chin nearly touched her chest. She knew better than to talk back, especially in front of others. Yao cared more about face than anything. Any word from her would only stoke the fire.

"I, Zhang Yao, have never stolen, never robbed anyone, no matter how poor I've been. I've always walked the straight path. And now look what I've raised—a son with sticky fingers. What a fine mother you are. Just look at the boy you've brought up."

Her mind detached from her body, as if floating above the scene, watching this farce unfold with cold indifference. She remembered praying over and over when she was pregnant with Ming, begging the heavens to show mercy and give her a son. She remembered carrying him on her back up into the hills to gather firewood. Every time she bent to chop a branch and straightened up, his little head would bump the back of hers. She always worried—had he gotten hurt?

"You call that parenting? Teaching a child isn't hard. If he doesn't listen, you beat him. And if he still doesn't listen, you beat him harder. That's how you raise a child. But you—you're soft. You can't bear to see him cry. That's why he's turned out like this."

The crowd outside grew larger. The whispers swelled.

Ling remembered when Ming had just learned to walk. He had pointed to the cupboard where she hid fruit candies, then to his mouth. She had taken out a candy, handed it to him, and shaken her head, saying, "That was the last one. All gone." Ming had smiled and taken the candy, and never pointed at the cupboard again. He'd always been such a gentle, thoughtful child.

Yao was still raging, his voice sharp, laced with contempt. His angry snorts, his scornful shaking of the head—he hurled words at her like stones, letting his fury tear through the room, as if burning away her "failings" would cleanse him. He needed this moment, this stage, to show everyone what a strict and righteous father he was—that the boy's failure wasn't his fault, but hers: the mother who couldn't stop doting.

Outside, the chatter faded into a hum, background noise. Ling's world fell silent, everything drowned out but Yao's voice, still ringing in her ears. It had always been like this—before, now, and likely always. No one had ever spoken for her, helped her, stood beside her. She was always alone, bearing every accusation in silence.

Eventually, Yao's voice quieted and stopped. The crowd began to disperse. The noise retreated into the distance.

Ling didn't move.

She didn't know how much time had passed—only that it felt endless. Her legs ached, knees bent, and the soreness had crept from her neck into her shoulders.

"It's late. You should get dinner started."

Yao's voice came again.

Ling kept her head down. Her thoughts were like a wasteland after a storm—stripped bare, nothing left to grasp. Something inside her had cracked, soundlessly. She lifted her foot and stepped toward the door. She didn't know where she was going. No—that wasn't true. There was only one place in her mind: the pond behind the house.

She felt Yao's grip clamp onto her arm—tight as an iron vise, locking her in place. She tried to pull away, but his strength overwhelmed hers. Her efforts were useless, like an ant trying to shake a tree. She wanted to walk out, but he dragged her back toward the bedroom. She felt like a weightless rag doll, hauled along until he pushed her down beside the bed.

"Sheng will make dinner. You rest here."

Without a glance back, Yao walked out and shut the door behind him.

Ling collapsed onto the bed and stared up at the mosquito net—white mesh squares, one after another, like an endless cage. She thought of ten years ago, when she followed Yao out of the mountain-ringed village. The hills were covered in blooming rhododendrons. In a hollow near Shenzhen, they cleared brush and built a mud-brick hut with their own hands. Winter wind slipped through the cracks in the walls. They lay under a stiff cotton quilt, shivering.

"Just a few more years," he said through chattering teeth. "I'll build you a house that keeps the wind out."

She had believed him.

For that promise, she worked through postpartum pain, bent over fields when she should've been resting. She survived on salted vegetables and plain porridge during the early days of the brick factory. Now, they had a solid brick house. Yao had become the respected Boss Zhang. But her life felt more like that old quilt—decent on the outside, cold to the bone.

She was tired. Too tired to fight anymore. All it would take was a short walk to the pond behind the house. One small step, and it would all be over. That simple.

Time dripped like wax, thick and slow. Outside, the light dimmed. She lay motionless, eyes wide open, as if even her breath had been drained. Only when the room was swallowed by darkness did she feel herself return—like surfacing from a long, suffocating submersion.

The house was silent. She was alone. Yao wasn't there.

She sat up and stepped barefoot onto the cold

tile floor. Quietly, she walked to the door. The turn of the knob sounded like a sigh.

The light in the living room was still on. In its harsh glow, Yao sat slouched on a stool by the front door, one leg stretched across the doorway, the other braced against the frame—forming a quiet barricade. His head drooped, arms folded across his chest. He looked asleep. Her heart sank. If she wanted to leave, she'd have to step over his leg. And he would wake.

He knew. He knew what she was thinking, where she might go. So he sat there, using the only thing left to him—his body—to block her way. He wouldn't apologize. Wouldn't soften. But this was how he told her: *You're not allowed to leave.*

Was she supposed to be moved by this? Why? Why should he think this was enough? That one door, one leg, could undo all the pain she'd swallowed over the years?

She clenched her jaw, turned back, and threw herself onto the bed.

That night, she drifted in and out of restless sleep, trapped in a haze of heavy, formless dreams. It wasn't until first light crept through the windows and the voices of early workers echoed in the courtyard that the mattress beside her finally dipped. Yao was back. He smelled faintly of cigarettes. Without a word, he lay down beside her.

And just like that, everything returned to where it had started.

She turned toward the wall and shut her eyes.

Just one more day, she told herself. *Today, Ming wants egg noodles.*

She couldn't leave.

At least… not yet.

The Boxer

Alexei Raymond

The Sunday-evening street blurred through reflections, movement, and unaided myopia. Habit kept him from missing his stop. His glasses were a short, acetate tie on his neck as he walked to his grandmother's apartment, carrying grave news. He greeted her and leaned in to be kissed on the right cheek. Each year it seemed he had to lean further down, as his grandmother's height diminished. Neither the twenty-seven-year-old grandson nor the seventy-four-year-old spoke beyond the greeting, as both took their seats at the table in the compact living room. Her silvery, corpulent cat was ignored. The grandson sat at the head of the table—bearer of bad news—perhaps the bad news itself. His grandmother was seated and cupped her soft face in a weathered hand. She regarded him as she would have had he been ten years old, freshly fallen, lightly scuffed, and seeking consolation.

"I, uh… we broke up. On Friday. I'm back at Mom's place. And, yeah."
"Why? What happened?"
Why indeed. He had not been able to admit to anyone who had not already known. He was not capable of the suicide inherent in it, nor the murder of the person they had seen him as. He took what breath he could.
"We've had a rough month, realized we had a lot of issues, tried to work through them—"
Because I'd had a three-month digital affair with a divorced woman halfway across the world.
"—and on Friday she concluded that she doesn't

want to keep trying and that, well," his chin quivered, and he felt choked. He struggled to still himself and not cry openly. When was the last time his grandmother had seen him cry? He couldn't recall. At the head of the table sat a ruin of a man seeking solace and a path forward without bringing down more of the world unto himself. He hoped no more questions would come, so no more lies would have to leave his mouth. The abrupt end of a nine-year relationship attracts questions like nothing else.

"So she just wanted to leave? Why?"
"She just started an exciting new job and she found a new circle of friends. And I was her first boyfriend, and she felt like—"
She couldn't forgive or trust me and time wouldn't heal any of it and she would always feel resentful, and I broke my image in her eyes and became unlovable.
When the deluge of excuses ceased and the patchwork of lies settled, he had a moment to recover his breath in the silence of his grandmother working to synthesize his words into understanding and judgement. To her, he was still a faultless, bright boy. Beloved, quiet, handsome. Wronged and left.
"But what issues did you have? You never complained about anything."
"I was just—I think I've been depressed this past year. Since we moved in together. I noticed how little she seemed to care about who I am, how disinterested she was, and it was hard to bear it daily. She noticed my state and it depressed her and—"
So I went roaming through the computer screen and

*found someone who cared the way I wanted to be
cared about.*

"That's not right. It's not good to keep things
inside. You were partners. And if that's what you
were going through, then it's for the best that it's
over. Then this had to happen. *God course-corrects
us.* She just wasn't meant for you and something
else is. I could always tell she wasn't too present.
Whenever you two visited, or when I visited you,
and then you stopped visiting me altogether,"
He sat, shoulders slumped, eyes fixed on an
indeterminate spot on the table. He tried to make his
grandmother's words fit into him somehow. Did
they make sense, even in the shadow of what had
truly happened? They did, somehow.

"When I was with your grandfather,"
Grandfather—the man whose very name was struck
through and little mentioned. All he'd known of a
grandfather he'd only seen twice in his life, was that
the man was a boxer, and that he'd left grandmother
for some undisclosed reason. His father's seething,
never-elucidated hatred for the man simmered
below the surface whenever the man was
mentioned. A coal of ashen anger glowed inside
him; it led to abandoning his father's surname.
Though they still told him, when he took up the
masculine sport in his teenage years: *your
grandfather was a boxer!* And the taking of the
mantle was a point of pride, and the invocation of a
distant grandfather as a boxer was one too.

"He always had so little patience for me. We
barely spoke. He used to come back from work
exhausted and mean, and it would always be a
disaster if I interrupted his rest."
For a moment, he forgot his own pain as family

history unfolded—one he had never heard before, and about so mysterious a character.

"One day he came back home from work in a bad mood and sat down on the couch in our living room. He was reading some book while I cleaned, and I accidentally brushed past him and moved his book. He beat me. He had no patience, and he thought I interrupted him on purpose. So, he used to beat me. And I used to blame myself for being clumsy and for disturbing him."

Her tone was steady, composed. She spoke of the previously untold episode with frustration, but the emotion there was far from raw. He wondered whether the family simply forgot to let him know, as the story clicked and reframed a lifetime. He listened.

"He was jealous. Always so jealous. He would always suspect me and question me about where I've been. There was a man who was a dear friend of mine, and a colleague on another occasion. They were really just friends. Nothing happened. And nosy neighbours only made it all worse. Poisoned him against me. And then one day I couldn't take any of it anymore and I took your father and your uncle, and I left him."

"Nobody ever told me. I didn't know." Regret washed over him for ever having met the man, though it happened innocently on a trip to Moscow to visit aunts and celebrate a 14th birthday. And he remembered the grey, diminutive man—spry, energetic, a head shorter than everyone else in his advanced age. The grandfather's unprompted, muddy excuses for why he hadn't been in touch. And above all he remembered how his father looked out at him from the grandfather's older

features. That distant man and the direct blood that
tied them.
"Well, it's not a nice story and your father doesn't
like to mention him."
"How old was he when it happened?"
"Oh, he was maybe five, and your uncle was only a
baby then. I'm telling you this to show that
sometimes things are meant to end. And whatever is
written for you is not with her."
"I understand. It's just—" to speak simple truths
hurts like nothing else, "It's just difficult."

He sipped at the tall glass of water she offered
and kept the same static view of a modest living
room, of the various signs of his grandmother's
profession as a seamstress. And as he drank, she
rummaged somewhere in her bedroom and returned
with a single yellowed photo.
"I think this is the only one I have left of him."
In the photo stood a group that seemed to be largely
unaware of a lens. Though he'd never seen the
grandfather in his youth, he immediately recognized
the load-bearing man in the photo whose features he
and his father bore. Curly hair, prominent ears, a
stern, handsome face—the young father held a
toddler whose face was hidden in the man's chest.
His father-to-be. Everyone in the photo, aside from
the toddler and his father, had their eyes cast
downwards, though the subject of their collective
gaze was outside the borders of the snapshot.

"This was taken at my father's funeral. We were
still together when he passed away. After I left your
grandfather, I tore up every photo I had of him. I
think I missed this one. Maybe I shouldn't have torn
them up."

Suddenly, he couldn't remember whether the man in the photo still lived. And after another moment, he recalled the faint news of his death, and how little anyone seemed to care. Next, he recalled the last time he'd seen the man, sometime in his later teens at a large family gathering the details of which he could barely make out. His grandfather had flown in from Moscow.

"I just remembered seeing him when he was here. How did you feel about it then?" His grandmother's eyes replayed scenes from that gathering.

"A lot of time passed since what happened, and when he was here, well. I didn't feel as strongly about it all. What do you remember?"

"Barely anything. I remember seeing him talking to family members. There were a lot of people, so I can't remember anything specific."

"Well, I didn't know if I even wanted your father to take me to that dinner, and your father didn't want to go there himself. And then I decided that to not come would be too rude, and my mother urged us to go. When your grandfather saw me there, he approached and immediately dropped to his knees. He begged for forgiveness. He was so thin—I think his cancer was advanced at that stage—and he just kept begging me for forgiveness. I told him that I forgive him and that was that. He then kneeled before my mother and begged her for forgiveness as well."

"You felt like you could? Forgive him, I mean."

"Yes, what else would I have done? To hold onto that anger my entire life? I just felt bad for him." She spoke with resignation, and the images that replayed in her mind seemed to fade. The grandson was brought back into view, sitting there, fighting the persistent urge to cry.

"I can't remember any of that."

"I think it happened before you arrived."

The grandfather's lone photograph lay between them, as he lay somewhere far away. And for a moment, his stern eyes seemed to look straight through the lens—and through him. Condemned, dead man—laid bare, forgiven, preserved in the perishable matter of a photo. His grandson's thoughts shot back to the night of the breakup, to the cold words he delivered to his broken beloved. *I want you to delete every single photo of me. Everything. Nothing. Nothing. And I will do the same.*

Once the matter of the old boxer was settled, his grandmother continued to console and assure the young one until he'd regained enough composure, at least enough to be able to make his way back home. He gave the silent cat a quick scratch behind the ear, then rose to stand by the door.

"Well. I'll go to the bus now. Thank you. I… Thank you." And before tears could gather and break surface tension, he leaned in once again and held his short grandmother. He felt her golden hands on his shoulders as she kissed him goodbye.

"It's for the best. It will be difficult, but remember that someone else is meant for you."

He thanked her with his weak voice, promised to return, and was back out in the unremarkable street.

What is to be done with these hands, this heart—its deeds and its shards?

He, bearing both his father's and grandfather's features, vanished in the mundane tangle of streets.

June Full Moon Special

Heart

Liam Johnson

The heart beats steady in its hollow chest,
A pulse that quickens with each passing breath.
It whispers secrets in a rhythmic thrum,
A silent drum that drums beneath the skin.

It pushes blood through silent, unseen halls,
A force that claims the space within the ribs.
No pause, no mercy in its steady march,
It claims its territory with every beat.

The ache can grow from quiet, subtle shifts,
A tightening grip that chills the marrow deep.
Each throb a subtle warning, a reminder,
That life can end in darkness, silent sleep.

The heart does not discern the line of life,
It simply moves, relentless, unafraid.
In every thump, a silent threat remains,
A quiet echo of what it can become.

Confession

Zary Fekete

PART I

You know exactly where she is…in the soft light of the coffee shop. She's bright when she answers the phone. Why not? She doesn't know why you're calling. The moment feels foreign. As if you're calling from another life.

Stay there, you say. *Wait.*

It's the first step onto a bridge you've never crossed. And though you've rehearsed this, your throat tightens at the idea of ever getting to the other side.

The drive is a blur. The road unwinds beneath you like an endless ribbon. You want to stop. But you know that if you stop, you'll never try this again.

PART II

She sits there. You want to sit there with her and speak of anything but this. You start with a smile and you immediately ditch it. Swap it for a more real face. One that won't fool her again.

Because you're a devil you actually catch yourself trying to weasel.

You whisper to yourself, "*It's not too late. You're a good liar.*"

But you've done that before and that path leads to a desert and you swallowed your last dram of water three weeks ago. No. Not quite right. Not water. And not weeks. What was it? Barely 30 minutes ago. Standard operating procedure for the last six months and before that the last 10 years as you've

been sliding down this slope…one with no bottom.
Unless you stop it here.

PART III
You stare at her and say it… and the words fall out
like stones. They hit the air and shatter. They come
out jagged. They strike her about the face and
throat.
Once they're out they're out. It's almost a relief.
The words. "Hiding…Lied…Drank…Liters…"
She mumbles a few questions.
You give her more words like vomit.
You imagine everything you ever drank pouring out
of your throat. Nice if it worked like that, right? Just
put it back where it came from. Undo it. Rewind it.
But this isn't Disney and spells aren't real.

PART IV
Is it weird to think of God now? Is this what He
meant? He said plenty of words, too. You
memorized some of them.
"Confess…Forgive…Cleanse…Justify…" Should
you say some of those?
No. She'd think you're playing her. Trying to soften
her up. After all, that's her Bible on the table. That's
how you knew she'd be here. Same place every day.
Coffee…tea…Psalms.
The next set of words don't work, and you can hear
yourself mouthing the script in return. "I'll do
better." (*wrong*) "This time it will be different." (*lie*)
"You deserve better." (*True…but where is he?*)
Instead, you pour out a deluge of pledges hoping
enough volume will kill the flame.

You promise again. And again. You beg for a different kind of cleansing, one that doesn't come from words but from some holy place.

PART V
You think about those words—*cleansed from all unrighteousness*. You think of the line between guilt and forgiveness.
Where are you on the line? Too close to the first to feel the second?
For the first time, maybe, you let the words sit before you. You don't try to bend them.

PART VI
And, in fact, that's where it started. Real healing. Years later, you can look back and say some new words to yourself.
"Sober…Six months…One year…Three years…"
And today the morning still starts at the coffee shop. But now the two of you are there together. She still has her Bible.
And you have one of your own.

Authors

MEL EINHORN won 1st Place of the Poetry Writing Contest. He is an octogenarian poet previously self-published two un-marketed unheralded poetry books. He won the American Academy of Poets Prize in college. He creates slice of life still life lyric poignant portrayals reflective of the beat era.
Headshot provided by Jenny Havens Photography.
Page 8

ALISON BRECHTEL is a writer and English teacher living in Chicagoland with her two children, 2 rescue dogs and husband. She graduated from Elmhurst University with an English degree specializing in journalism. Her work has appeared in *Empyrean, Screamin Mamas*, and *The B(e)aring All Project.*
Page 40

SAMUEL BROWN.
Page 24;

KAYLYN DUNN.
Page 36

ZARY FEKETE grew up in Hungary. He has a debut novella, *Words on the Page,* out with DarkWinter Lit Press and a short story collection, *To Accept the Things I Cannot Change: Writing My Way Out of Addiction,* out with Creative Texts. He enjoys books, podcasts, and many many many films.
Page 73

TALIESIN GORE lives in an annexe in his mother's garden and works night shifts as a care worker. His poetry has appeared in many publications, in print and online, including *Littoral Magazine, Reach Poetry* and *Stimulus Respond.* His fiction can be found at *MetaStellar, East of the Web* and elsewhere.
Page 44; 55

LIAM JOHNSON.
Page 72

EMMA KIM.
Page 52

FINLEY PARKER has many published works across numerous magazines. He is currently working on a novel set to publish summer of 2026.
Page 28

ALEXEI RAYMOND is a writer whose work explores post-Soviet diasporic lives, moments of threshold, and fractured identities. Originally from the Middle East, he is currently based in Belgrade. His stories appear in *The Bloomin' Onion, Lowlife Lit Press*, and *The Crawfish*, with forthcoming work in *Blood+Honey, Waffle Fried*, and *The Argyle Literary Magazine*.
Page 65

MICHAEL ROQUE, born and raised in Los Angeles, discovered his love for poetry and prose amid friends on the bleachers of Pasadena City College. Now he currently lives in the Middle East and is being inspired by the world around him. His poems have been published by literary magazines like *North Dakota Quarterly, Cholla Needles, The Literary Hatchet* and others.
Page 23; 27; 35; 38

LUKE REUTEMAN is a part-time poet from Milwaukee, WI where he works as a hydrogeologist for the state. He's best outdoors, where most of his poetry is written.
Page 37; 42; 54

WYATT STRAWBRIDGE is a casual Quaker, writer, and editor, born originally in Chicago and living in Haverford, PA. Wyatt is a sophomore English and Russian double major at Kenyon College, an editor for Lyceum Magazine, and has work forthcoming in Corporeal Magazine.
Page 22; 26

AVERY WALKER.
Page 21

HARPER WELLS is a Christian poet from Idaho.
Page 10

MEGAN WILDHOOD is a writer who helps her readers feel seen in her monthly newsletter, poetry chapbook Long Division (Finishing Line Press, 2017), her full-length poetry collection Bowed As If Laden With Snow (Cornerstone Press, May 2023) as well as Mad in America, The Sun and elsewhere. You can learn more about her at meganwildhood.com.
Page 11

DOUGLAS YOUNG is an author and professor emeritus whose essays, poems, and short stories have appeared in a variety of publications in America, Canada, and Europe. His first novel, *Deep in the Forest*, was published in 2021 and the second, *Due South*, came out in 2022. His first book of essays, *This Little Opinion Plus $1.50 Will Buy You a Coke: A Collection of Essays*, appeared in 2024.
Page 30

HUINA ZHENG, a Distinction M.A. in English Studies holder, works as a college essay coach. Her stories have been published in *Baltimore Review, Variant Literature, Midway Journal,* and others. Her work has received nominations three times for both the Pushcart Prize and Best of the Net. She resides in Guangzhou, China with her family.
Page 58

Sponsored by Kada's Bookstore

Kada's Bookstore is an editing and publishing company founded by author, Kaylyn Marie Dunn. Formed in 2021, Kada's Bookstore believes that anyone can be a successful writer. All it takes is a story and pen. Once those words find paper then the possibilities open up!

Kada's Bookstore is dedicated to teaching authors how to self-publish their novels and actually get their books in the hands of readers who will read them. Additionally, Kada's Bookstore also acts as a publishing house. For those who only want to focusing on the writing, Kada's Bookstore is here to do the heavy lifting!

For more information go to www.kadasbookstore.com

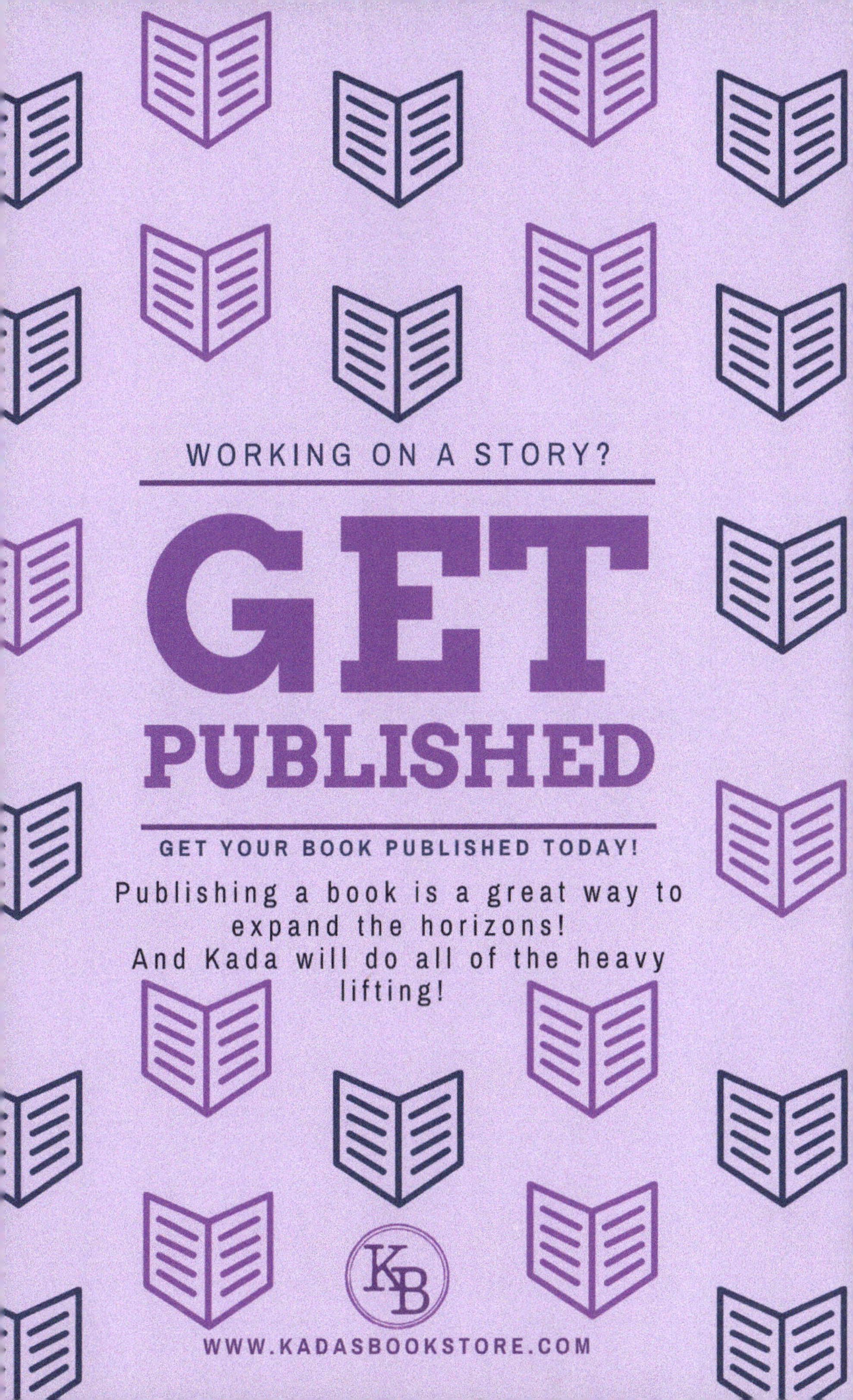

WORKING ON A STORY?

GET
PUBLISHED

GET YOUR BOOK PUBLISHED TODAY!

Publishing a book is a great way to expand the horizons!
And Kada will do all of the heavy lifting!

KB

WWW.KADASBOOKSTORE.COM